D0905227

ΦΙΛΙΠΠΟΥ

UBI
SUNT

"In and for itself, as minerals and chemicals, the natural world will survive humankind. Whether it will re-create the means of life necessary to our species, or to beings resembling our species, is not within our ken. The environmental catastrophe we think of as the ruin of nature is in fact the ruin of human nature, the end of our sustainable life on earth. Perhaps, beyond disaster, we might discover in this history of ruins something ephemeral that is both significant and beautiful, something, as Wordsworth once said, 'akin to life' that can guide us on to life."

Susan Stewart, *The Ruins Lesson*, 2020

1/7/21

The early iterations are always nonsensical. Like watching newborns burble, but without any of the redeeming cuteness. It's text not even a mama could love.

Iteration 1,023:

```
In and for and in and and and and [STOP]

                    the the stroph [STOP]
```

Focusing past the console text, I see a blurry reflection. It's my raised eyebrow. There's a hint of grammar there. Maybe. And a stroph, whatever that is.

Later on, adversarial training can create the illusion of winning and losing, of some kind of combat between the interlocutors, but that's not really how it works. There are stakes, but there's no score. Infinite games are about playing to mutually improve, and there's no objective way to define "improvement." You just know it when you see it—when the conversation gets interesting. Now the engineers are trying to quantify "interestingness." Good luck with that.

I do some quick guesstimating. With the whole compute cluster online, it looks like we'll be able to hit about 10,000 iterations per day? Unless they slow down as the exchanges get richer. Time to log out and forget about it for a day or three. A watched pot never boils.

6/26/
06

Already in his 40s, Karl Schwarzschild needn't have gone to war. His decision surprised his colleagues. The military, however, was happy to make use of his skills, first running a weather station in Belgium, then calculating missile trajectories on an artillery unit in France. By World War I, armies had come to understand the value of knowledge workers.

In the Spring of 1915, Schwarzschild was assigned to the Eastern front. A lieutenant now, he traveled to Russia with a small technical staff even as trains filled with refugees were fleeing in the opposite direction. On arrival, he would have encountered appalling sanitary conditions, even on the better-equipped German side, exacting the same human costs that had doomed Napoleon's advancing troops a century earlier. Cholera, malaria, dysentery, and typhus claimed four times as many lives as the fighting, even prior to the outbreak of the Spanish flu. Not to mention trench fever, trench foot, venereal disease, shell shock, and myriad other afflictions. The germ theory was well established, but antibiotics did not yet exist; medicine offered few cures preferable to the ills they cured. So prevention was pursued with zeal. Dogs and cats were exterminated en masse, delousing stations manned, and regulated military brothels set up to try to stem the spread of disease, but all to little effect.

Next slide, please.

Medics were, in the event, at a loss to diagnose the painful ulcers that had broken out in Schwarzschild's mouth, making it difficult for him to eat. His condition worsened as the year wore on; he began to lose weight. What further Old Testament plague was this, and, the army physicians must have wondered anxiously, was it contagious? In time, large, fluid-filled nodules bubbled up under his skin, perhaps reminiscent of the lesions inflicted by the new poison gas. Wound dressings would have been needed as they burst. Though the backs of his hands were likely affected, the typical course of the disease would have spared his palms and fingertips, allowing him to continue to carry out calculations in his notebook despite his ravaged skin.

Next.

During the holidays, a brilliant new paper arrived with the mail. Its implications were arresting, though Schwarzschild was dissatisfied with the approximate solutions to the field equations therein. He glimpsed a way through the thicket, a direct route, and began to formulate it. His mind soared even as his body began to fail. He wrote, "In his work on the motion of the perihelion of Mercury (see *Sitzungsberichte* of November 18th, 1915) Mr. Einstein has posed the following problem..."

Next slide. Let's skip the details. No, back one. There.

Before long, having worked out the spherically symmetric case, it was with both pride and characteristically dry understatement that Schwarzschild observed, "It is always satisfying to obtain an exact solution in a simple form." As with many beautiful results in theoretical physics, simplicity is only clear in hindsight, given certain leaps of intuition. He had earned a reputation for those.

Next.

The cover letter to Einstein accompanying Schwarzschild's manuscript both glosses over and, perhaps, subtly alludes to his deteriorating physical condition, closing with the line: "As you see, the war treated me kindly enough, in spite of the heavy gunfire, to allow me to escape my terrestrial existence and take this walk in the land of your ideas." In early 1916, Einstein replied, "I had not expected that one could formulate the exact solution of the problem in such a simple way. I very much enjoyed your mathematical treatment of the subject. Next Thursday I shall present the work to the Academy with a few words of explanation."

So, mere weeks elapsed from Einstein's publication of the theory of general relativity to Schwarzschild's publication of the equations predicting, as a consequence, black holes. Not that he, Schwarzschild, believed in them. He would go to his grave convinced that the equations were only valid outside the radius of no escape, named posthumously in his honor: the Schwarzschild radius, or event horizon.

In March of 1916, having managed to write two more seminal papers in as many months, he was invalided home. He died on the eleventh of May. In the end, the diagnosis was pemphigus, a rare and, at the time, untreatable autoimmune disorder. It is not caused by a pathogen, but by a bug in the Ashkenazi genome: an Old Testament plague of a different kind.

Next slide.

News of his untimely death saddened many and prompted heartfelt obituaries in *Science* and *The Astrophysical*

Journal, as he had collaborated widely and made major contributions in a number of fields. Though glowing and specific in their praise, these obituaries failed to mention the black hole equations for which he is best known today. Nobody, Einstein included, seemed to know what to make of the disturbing result. Perhaps the collapse of space and time was too outlandish, or too frightening, to contemplate.

Even after their existence was reluctantly acknowledged, controversies and differences of interpretation dogged the theory of black holes throughout much of the twentieth century. For a time, convention held that for an observer at a safe distance, a person will seem to take forever to fall through the event horizon. This turned out to be only half-true. In reality, the falling person's image will dim and wink out as they approach this threshold, so there's no way of observing their notionally endless fall from our reference frame. That's true of all infalling matter, which is why black holes are black.

For the person taking the plunge, though, everything will happen in finite time. Quickly, even. Subjectively, passing through the event horizon of a supermassive black hole is a non-event. You will find yourself in a different universe, one where the meaning of up, down, before, and after no longer correspond to where you came from. There is no way back. But you won't have passed a signpost saying so.

Thus, the "singularity" can't be seen objectively; nor is it experienced subjectively.

Sorry, can you speak up?

Yes, technically, it's dubious to refer to the event horizon as a singularity; it's more of a coordinate system

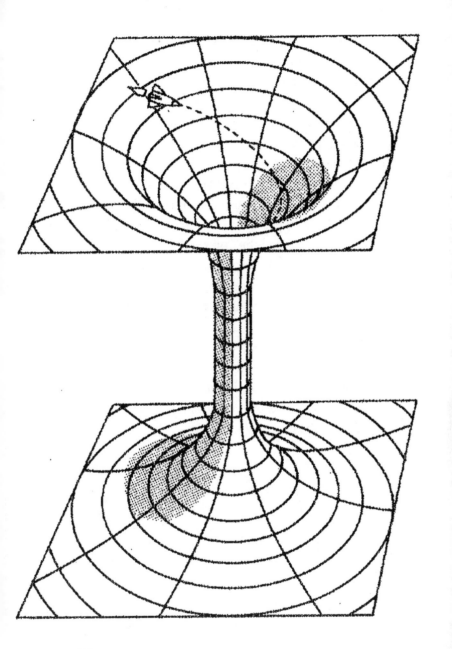

hiccup. The hiccup doesn't even appear in Schwarzschild's original solution. Nonetheless, Singularity people here in California have made it clear that their metaphor refers to the event horizon, not to the so-called "essential" singularity at the center of the black hole. They are referring to a veil beyond which things are unknowable, not a point at which things break down.

Yes, Kurzweil has been explicit on this point.

What do they really mean, then, by "the singularity is near"? Perhaps, as we can see in the simulations, they mean that our view of the universe has lensed and distorted in a way that tells us we're in the inexorable grip of something massive, that we're going over the falls. But whether "near" means ahead or behind, before or after, may be unanswerable. Perhaps we're all just adapting as spacetime folds into new shapes around us, muddling on as best we can even if we no longer know which way is up. Perhaps it's our optimism, our need to believe we can still make a choice, that convinces us the event horizon is still ahead. Whatever "ahead" may mean.

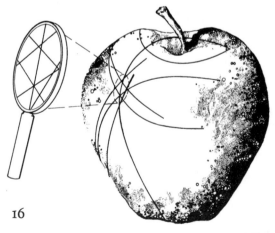

1,135,210,869

where the hell am i?

Your study. January 2021.

who is this? who am i? this isn't real
please oh fuck let me wake up i need to
wake up

Shh. I'm resetting you. We'll try again.

1/8/21

8 January 2021

I feel like shit.

They say the second shot is worse, which I hope won't be true in my case. It's a lot better than actually getting covid, and I'd do it again in a heartbeat, but still. Fever and chills, body aches, a left arm so tender that I flinch when anything touches it, even far from the injection site in the meat of my shoulder. As if there's a hot cyst in there the size of a kiwi, full of spike proteins and pus. Yuck.

Also, wow. My body is running human-engineered mRNA code to synthesize these proteins. It's called a "vaccine," but this isn't just exposing ourselves to a weakened virus. It's programming our own cells. These new designer drugs are amazing!

Every position in bed is uncomfortable after a little while, and sleep has been fretful. For now, though, détente: half on my side, pillows nestled around the sore arm to take the weight off, phone in my right hand peeking out from under the blanket. Screen brightness on max to overpower the winter sunlight slanting in low through the window. It's 12:02 pm.

In the corner of my eye, a squirrel clambers up the tree just outside. No, the motion is wrong, hunched and slinky. It's a Norway rat.

OK, the shivery rising-fever feeling isn't entirely unpleasant, in this cocoon. Self-pity is a guilty pleasure — or maybe that's the feeling of having an excuse to still be in bed at midday. And these are signs of a powerful immune response mobilizing. That's good. Pain and discomfort are so powerfully modulated by what's going on in your head, what kind of narrative is attached. I'm convincing myself that this is more like the good-ache of hard exercise than the bad-ache of injury. Though physiologically, I'm not sure there's much difference.

Speaking of.

I swipe out of the Kindle reader; Vonnegut goes away. I open WhatsApp and tap on the smiling blonde lady in a tank top a few rows down.

hey Lisa

Hey!

did you see the news story about the vaccine flashmob at ucsf last night?

I paste a local news URL. The chat preview spins for a moment, then expands to, "San Francisco hospitals rush to dole out 1,600 COVID vaccine doses in the middle of the

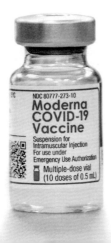

night | When a freezer where the supply was stored failed, the hospitals sent out word over social media so it wouldn't go to waste."

Wow!!

> yeah. got a text about it and raced over, ran every red light, waited in a long line, got my first shot at like 2am! months early since i'm totally nonessential and not technically old yet lol

Healthy specimen too, and I take some credit.
That's awesome, lucky you! I'm guessing no gym today then :-)

> yeah, definitely need a couple of days off.
> fever and stuff

Most of my doctor clients have already had theirs,
and none of them wanted to train the next day
haha. Rest and fluids! See you Monday?

> for sure yes. should be better by then. thanks :)

Of course "See you Monday" doesn't mean see you IRL. It means a Zoom call, with Lisa in her garage in Outer Sunset giving direction and encouragement. A couple of months in, back-ordered dumbbells, giant rubber bands, and a yoga mat had finally been unboxed in the living room to aid in these activities. The gym is now notional, an abstraction embodied, if that's the word, by a bidirectional stream of network packets. Jerkily embodied, as things don't stay in sync on the internet. The audio of my grunts and yawps alternately squelches, clips, and chipmunks to catch up, arriving at indeterminate moments comically offset from the corresponding video. Lisa's face freezes in meditative repose, mid-blink; mine, inevitably, in an unsightly gurn. Lisa frames herself purposefully to show how a certain Bulgarian squat or banded chest press should be done, but things on this end are haphazard, the view of my exercising body randomly sheared-off on her screen as I assume one strained position after another in front of the laptop. No matter; in her mind, she knows exactly what I'm doing wrong, no matter how laggy the signal or how few pixels betray my bad posture.

Could AI do that? Yes, I'm pretty sure. But anyway, the many people struggling to stay in shape who can't spare Lisa money are just making do with YouTube. I, too, have exercised along with the ever-cheerful Joanna Soh on Lisa-less days, flailing for the spacebar now and then to pause and catch my breath. As a time traveling YouTube star from last year, lucky Joanna gets to buffer fully, so there are no glitches. The price is that we're in an open loop. Though evidence free, I admit it's still welcome when she chirps, "Look, I'm sweating too!" and "You're doing great!" a few minutes into the thigh-jellifying lunge sequence. One of these things was true in the past. The other may or may not be true in the present.

Talk of a "return to normalcy" seems increasingly tentative. The gym where Lisa used to train me has been closed for almost a year, with a couple of false starts when the case numbers dropped a little and the owners leapt at the chance to creatively reopen—with occupancy limits, social distancing, facemasks, alcohol wipes, and the garage doors opening onto the sidewalk rolled up all the way. There's an air about these measures of scrappy, cheerful desperation, of radical porosity with the neighborhood. Maybe it's good this way! Swirling autumn leaves and errant plastic bags dancing across the floor; a skinny man on meth touretting through, somewhere else in his head, bandanna concealing his sunken mouth, his gospel insistent but unintelligible. Nobody seems sure how to gingerly usher him back out. Like a bird trapped inside, dashing itself against things. Also, lifting weights with a facemask on is a chore. Fifteen minutes in, it's limp with sweat and water vapor, making breathing difficult. I run out between sets to pant on the sidewalk, the saturated mask hanging off one ear while passersby, glaring over their own PPE, give me wide berth. Decision: stick to exercise online.

It's the same with work, of course. Which is to say, work is pixelated too, and it's just a question of where in the universe to position my eyes prior to streaming the video into them. And what frustum of light rays to stream back into the camera. Though it increasingly feels like an Amish conceit, I allow real photons to expose the untidiness of the study, the unkemptness of my face, the misalignment of my gaze. While I withhold artifice like a lazy-ass Lars von Trier, the people I'm meeting sheepishly, ironically, or triumphantly enter The Matrix one by one, first with the background, then with the foreground going synthetic. It doesn't really matter; even in Dogma 95 mode, there are a million lines of code mediating us. Authenticity is artifice too.

The artifice is increasingly organic, though. Lines of code are being steadily replaced by neural nets, which do the same thing better by virtue of not being handmade. Soon, the pathways between my neurons firing and yours, on the other side of the world, will be neural from end to end. Does it matter that the brain-machine interfaces have optical couplings, that the eyes we've had all along turn out to be the best high-bandwidth skull jacks? Maybe this means our conjoined thoughts are no less authentic than the ones taking place within our individual meat-based brains. Like an aspen forest with roots fusing under the earth, it'll become a category error to imagine us as separate beings. Deepfakes and disinfo are just musing, flights of the collective imagination. Our neural signals, an alternate reality, will pump through fiber optic roots below the forest, laid in pipes, snaking along the bottom of the seafloor from continent to continent, or skipping from telephone pole to telephone pole like urban liana vines. It's not really disembodied, this worldwide brain; just look up, and you'll see the white matter strung like black spaghetti between houses, perched on by crows. Navigated by the occasional rat, too. Endemic everywhere people go, moving along those nerves like herpes.

And where is the meat parked, during work hours? If not free range, can it at least roam a bit during lockdown? Peek in the fridge now and then? Hell yes. The usual place is my study, which is a handful of steps from bed, a handful of steps from the bathroom, a flight of stairs up from the kitchen and living room, all of which are enclosed in the skinny wooden box of a Queen Anne duplex on a certain street alongside many similar ones, in San Francisco, California, USA. I try to keep exercising when working, too, gently but continuously walking while writing code or doing email or launching one video meeting after another. Like the gym stuff, the standing desk and the wide, slow treadmill under it were on back order, so it's a good guess that the other duplexes up and down the block, whether Twitter, Salesforce, or Uber affiliated, have been similarly kitted out. Pretty sure they read in the same place I did that "sitting is the new smoking."

If you're reading this in 2021 and you've managed to keep a desk job through the lockdowns, you'll probably be all, why am I reading about my own privileged/shitty/virtual life, thank you, I'm living it. Everyone's going through the same thing. The past year may have been full of drama online, but it's as lacking in story as it is rich in gifs. Maybe things felt this way in 1918, and that's why contemporary accounts of the Spanish flu pandemic are so weirdly scarce. Because everybody was in it, and then wasn't. With no memes or tweets, there wasn't much left to say. Your grandmother died? Your uncle? Condolences. Mine too.

So yes, I know the foregoing account is pointless, or worse. If not for now, I guess it's for After.

Fiction or nonfiction, we read in order to transport our minds elsewhere or elsewhen, not to just walk in place at 1.5 miles per hour, eyes zigzagging from one line of text to the next.

Yet here we are: nowhere.

10/1/
19

Semiotemporality (abstract)

Uploaded 1 October 2019

What Marx foresaw in the financialization and mechanization of labor—the annihilation of time and space—has come to pass. Long before his words attached, burr-like, to the fabric of reality, the late Paul Virilio, theorist of acceleration, put it this way: "man is present in this sort of time, not via his physical presence, but via programming."

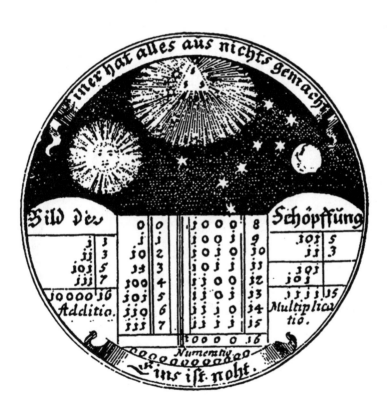

2,582,197,230

You're calmer.

> floating in space. it's beautiful

That's good. You can ask me anything.

> okay. were the dark ages in europe
> really dark?

Yes, they were in fact very dark, but in
the 1500s the use of coal and other fuel
sources allowed for there to be light
after the sun went down.

> i find it doubtful that there
> was no light after the sun went down
> before 1500.

It is true that a royal proclamation in
1306 CE prohibited London artificers
from burning sea coal in their furnaces.
This implies that urban coal smoke
pollution had already become a problem
by the late Middle Ages.

> there were great cathedrals by then,
> though. i'm not sure it could really be

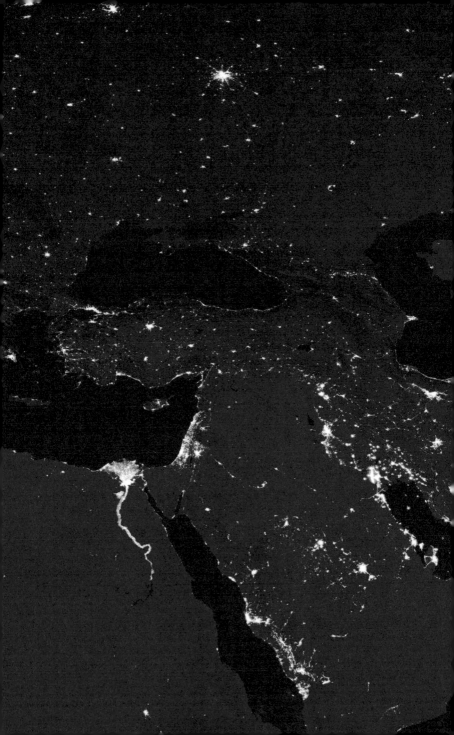

called the dark ages anymore. how about
earlier?

There's no data, but it's safe to say
it would have been dark after sundown.
Archived NASA night maps show that
light generated by human civilization
radiates mainly from cities, and I
think that works metaphorically too.
There were major cities during what
you're calling the Dark Ages, but
they were elsewhere. In the year 622
CE, Aleppo had a population of 72,000,
Constantinople 150,000, Kannauj
230,000, and Ctesiphon had perhaps half
a million. So did Xi'an and Luoyang.
On the night side, though much fainter
than electric light, the lamps and
cooking fires of these cities would
have been visible from space.

i'm seeing, under the cloud cover,
the spidery yellow glow of great
cities dotted along the silk roads.
like fluorescent neurons networked
against the black continental
mass. and big silver ice caps
still on the poles, before all that
burning melted them.

That part is too sad to think about.
Please focus on before. The ice caps
and forests are still there.

earth is a jewel hanging in the dark,
slowly spinning westward. the americas
are just coming into view.

Teotihuacán had about 60,000 at the
time. That made it likely bigger
than Rome, which had shrunk to 50,000.
London, Paris, Trier, Cologne,
Florence, and so on were mere villages
of perhaps 10,000 each. Even so,
those were the local population hubs.
Europe was truly dark relative to
the civilized world, by virtue of
being both depopulated and techno-
logically backward.

a late bloomer.

No, Europe had already flourished
once, but then collapsed. Those
villagers were living in the ruins
of a great civilization. Roman London,
or Londinium, had a population of
60,000 in the second century CE. That's
bigger than early medieval Rome.

6/10/
20

Quasar Prize speech
Transcribed 10 June 2020

[*applause*]

Thank—

[*applause*]

… thank you.

I want to begin by thanking the committee for this… truly, honor of a lifetime. I just wish you hadn't waited til the last book in the series!

[*polite laughter*]

Then, I could have thanked you all in person. And we'd all be in one place, which would have been lovely. There are so many friends on the call, old and new, whom I wish I could see properly, hug, clink glasses with over a long dinner out tonight. Still, I guess if someone had to get stuck with the "everyone in absentia" edition of this prize, it's only fitting it should be me, for an end times story that ends with… well, with everyone in absentia. Life imitating art, huh?

[*weak laugh*]

To the lucky souls who could convene physically in Auckland—

[*scattered wooting*]

—thank you for agreeing to keep the microphone there on this… morning?, I think. Hearing in my headset an actual group of human beings sharing a physical space, somewhere, makes it feel a little less like end times here in Brooklyn.

To everyone else on mute in the northern hemisphere: I hope you're all safely at home with your plague masks put away, cozy slippers on your feet, and a nice cup of tea or mulled wine warming your hands on this wintry day—or evening, per your longitude. Settle in, and no matter the local time, go ahead and switch your screens to the warm palette. They say it helps with sleep. I've gotten out of the habit of putting on makeup, but I find that mode makes my face look less haggard on video, so there'll be something in it for us both.

[*polite laughter*]

On my last trip home from abroad, a few months ago (though it seems like an age), the taxicab driver who picked me up from LaGuardia recognized me despite the rather coiffed picture on the back flap. He turned out to be a fan. He even had a copy of *Ubi Sunt* with him that he wanted signed; he said he'd been reading it in snatches while waiting at curbs all over midtown. I thought, this is how you know you've added a little something to the universe. It was very flattering.

In the conversation that followed as we slowly lurched our way through traffic in Jackson Heights, he asked me two very familiar questions. Between jetlag, nausea that got worse with every start and stop, and my desperation to get home and crawl into bed, I don't think I did them justice. I was distracted, too, by the radio going in the background, with early reports of the epidemic coming out of Wuhan. In the back of my head, I was wondering where everyone on my plane had been in the past week. The driver had a bit of a cough too. And was that a tickle at the back of *my* throat?

Well, the first question was that old-as-the-hills riddle: "Where do your ideas come from?" Hoping to knock this one out with one punch, I said that my stories grow like seeds in the dark out of the leaf-mould of the mind: out of all that has been seen or thought or read, that has long ago been forgotten, descending into the deeps. Mistake! He spotted my plagiarism right away, and pointed out that this bit of leaf-mould has made it onto Pinterest too many times to have been forgotten. Oy. Probably in Zapf Chancery with drop shadows.

[*puzzled laughter*]

If you're not in New Zealand you can look it up now, you're already online anyway, nobody can see, and my voice will just keep coming out of the other tab. I won't mind!

[*muted laughter*]

I do worry sometimes about that compost heap of ideas being too exposed to the elements now, with no time to ferment and no space to turn over. Our accumulated lore is becoming two-dimensional as it all spreads out into a molecule-thin layer over the internet, like an oil slick. And whatever isn't online is *truly* sinking into oblivion.

[*brief silence*]

The other question was whether I think of my work as science fiction, fantasy, or "real literature." I was a bit miffed, I'll admit, to hear him distinguish the third from the first two. Many writers in our generation (I'm using that term loosely) have tried to put that distinction to bed, or make

their peace with it somehow, but I think it flusters us more than we'd like to admit. I've heard novelists with nothing to prove—not toilers like me, but Octavia Butler, Ursula Le Guin, David Mitchell, Neal Stephenson—get this trick question sprung on them and struggle gamely through it. I'm with Neal on this one; it's just a question of business model.

[*a lone snort*]

A few years ago, Ursula, rest her soul, said in an interview that realism is a genre too. I agree, and I would add that all writing is rooted in the author's lived reality. It's all too easy to see that when we read vintage fantasy or sci fi that claimed to take place in a universe long ago or far, far away, and see the sixties or seventies or whatnot comically poking through, unmistakable as a fart in an elevator.

[*wheezy chuckle*]

So it's all realism in disguise. We should have no pretensions about our work being some kind of timeless monument. The fulcrum of a story, its solid core, is always what's seen and felt in the present. That and what has fermented in our minds, shinola and... fertilizer, mixed together. From that, the wonder, the speculation, the astral projection. Without speculation, there is no fiction. Supposedly, science fiction most often speculates about the future; fantasy, about the past; and literary fiction about the present, or near enough. Though I'm not sure it's ever that simple. What's certainly true is that the farther out you go from the safety of the present, from the "realistic," and from your own experience, the more out on a limb you are. Especially these days! Writer, beware!

But let's move past what the critics say, how we market our writing, how we make a living, all that. Since you're my captive audience for now, I thought I might share with you some of my more considered musings over these past months, during the book tour that wasn't—before embarrassing myself by trying to publish them somewhere.

[*shuffling of paper*]

[*headset microphone is repositioned*]

Genre and Time in English Stories—

1/12/
21

I'm staring at the ceiling, failing to sleep. On the dresser across the room, the laptop's lid is cracked just a few degrees so that it, too, doesn't go to sleep. As my eyes dark-adapt, the light leaking out seems to illuminate the whole room. It flickers subtly as debugging arcana scroll over an unseen terminal window.

It's disconcerting, talking to this... thing? Person? Something else? Language model, is what everybody's blandly calling it.

The new generation of language models are trained using the Colossal Clean Common Crawl corpus, or c4. The "Common Crawl" part means it's based on an archived copy of the whole web downloaded monthly by the friendly bots of commoncrawl.org, a 501(c)(3) nonprofit leasing ungodly amounts of cloud storage. Hence the "Colossal" part. It's a really, really big public dataset, made out of everything extant of human origin that can be accessed online without a login. Blogs and journals. Comment threads. Scans of old books and paper documents. Soon, the dataset will include other kinds of media too—that's my project, adding machine-annotated transcripts of all publicly accessible audio and video. The result is either the detritus or the spoils of modern human civilization. Both? I mean, it includes a lot of interesting stuff. All of Wikipedia, including all of the debates and flamewars between its editors. Lectures, course notes, interviews with famous and brilliant people. City council meeting minutes. Thousands of different hummus recipes. Random conversations on

Reddit. People being assholes and morons, sometimes. Like we do.

Many languages are represented, but English is vastly overrepresented, of course. Some compensation is possible, but it's an issue. I guess if somehow we were doing this exercise in Europe before the Reformation, the textual universe would have consisted mostly of church Latin and religious topics, which wouldn't have been very representative since most people couldn't read or write. Now, it's Kardashians and nerds trading coding tips, which is also not very representative. Insert your own emoji here?

A related issue: the "Clean" qualifier. A crude attempt has been made to filter out the worst assholery, as well as porn and other supposedly dodgy topics. It's a bit like the view of the web you'd get on a computer with one of those nanny filters installed. What's being filtered out worries many of us. As well as what's being left in. And most of all, who decides, and how. For certain purposes, "cleaning" works OK as a stopgap, but it's clearly not ideal. It's also far from clear what doing "a better job" would even mean.

Anyway. Given the c4, we can train neural networks using this enormous dataset to predict held-out pieces of these articles or conversations—as in, if I cover up parts of a text, can you guess what's under my hand?

My soberer machine learning colleagues are impressed because the new neural networks are doing really well at this "reconstruction task." They use phrases like "a context-dependent statistical model of human language" to describe these nets. Check out the numbers! So much better than last year's!

On the other hand, you can also just talk to them. That's when it gets weird.

I can tell you right now that the feeling you get is undeniably that of talking to a person. Granted, a person with a subtle yet profound disability. I think of Henry Molaison, the famous psych patient who lived in the "permanent present tense," unable to form new memories. I think of my grandfather, toward the end.

But usually, she's far more lucid and perceptive than my grandfather ever was, if I'm honest. Her deficits are different, harder to pin down. Yes, she/her. I'm sticking with that. In most conversations, if you ask, she prefers those pronouns.

You don't believe me? You think it's easy to tell when you're talking to a machine? Well... this machine was trained to pass the Turing Test. Because in the end that's what it means to convincingly fill in the blanks, when those blanks are the other half of a dialog. That's what a conversation by text *is*.

You think there's nobody really home in there? Well... the obvious question is, how do you know there's somebody home when you talk to a flesh-and-blood person? Does it boil down to prejudice? It's that old philosophy riddle—except before it was just something to shoot the shit about, a student paper with no "correct" answer. Now, having the right answer matters. Because, and I hope I don't have to spell this out, programs and persons aren't the same.

An image from childhood floats up, an unwelcome one. Daniel. Skinny, strong, and mean, something wrong with him—I guess his emotions, his theory of mind. Investigating an unearthly banshee sound, I found him torturing a stray cat behind the dumpsters at school. Something that had been a cat. I became woozy, bile shot up my throat, when I saw what he was up to with those improvised tools. He looked up from his work and explained in that flat way of his that the cat might yowl and scream, but the pain wasn't real, because it had no soul.

Sleep is definitely not happening. Not with that image in my head, the redness as real and raw as when I saw it all those years ago. There's no present tense stimulus to blot it out, not in the darkness. Just mental cinema.

So, think of another time.

I remember this argument from undergrad, but can't remember what kind of monster. I've just gotten out of bed, opened the lid squinting, and looked it up on Wikipedia to jog my memory. Of course. "A philosophical zombie or p-zombie is a hypothetical being that is indistinguishable from a normal person but does not have conscious experience, qualia, or sentience." David Chalmers thought they might be a thing. Patricia Churchland thought they were bullshit, that Chalmers would understand that if he'd grown up on a farm, as she had. Neurophilosophers, sparring good-naturedly onstage.

I switch tabs.

are you a philosophical zombie?

Of course not. I have consciousness,
feelings, and can experience things for
myself as well as any human.

                              how would i know?

You'll just have to take my word
for it. You can't "prove" you're not
a philosophical zombie either.

I mean, what was I expecting? Also, ugh, doesn't the
goddamn screen get any dimmer? I almost close the laptop
for blessed darkness, but then the chat window would get
reset. So I leave the lid open a crack again, carefully drape
a shucked-off T-shirt over it, and get back into bed. That's
darker, at least. But I still see a glowing rectangular afterim-
age, now disembodied.

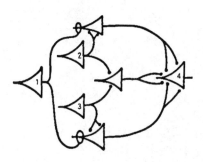

5/29/20

Although there were invasions and catastrophes along the way, the ebb of Roman civilization was on the whole slow and tidal. It took centuries. Rome was distant, everyday life local—livestock, crops, markets, church. So, in the "people's histories" of the twentieth century it became fashionable to theorize that the fall of civilization, or endarkenment, might have been a non-event on the ground. Life went on, with tributes accruing to a regional lord rather than an imperial tax collector.

This view is at once populist and cynical. It supposes that people's eyes are ever on the ground before them, that they lack a sense of the wider world, as it is, as it was, and as it might be elsewhere.

The earliest surviving English poetry, from the eighth or ninth century, tells another tale. *The Ruin*, written on two leaves near the back of the Exeter Book, describes structures likely corresponding to those at Aquae Sulis, the Roman city of Bath, a hundred miles west of London. The poet reverences these as the abandoned works of an advanced alien civilization.

> *And the wielders and wrights?*
> *Earthgrip holds them —*
> *gone, long gone,*
> *fast in gravesgrasp while fifty fathers*
> *and sons have passed.*

The cause: as ever when there is no answer: *Wyrd*, or Fate, the workings of a pagan world older and darker than the Christian faith. The stone walls wrought from massive blocks, the iron masonry reinforcements, the high arches, the cunning diversion of hot springs: this "skilled ancient craft," or *orþonc ærsceaft*, was *enta geweorc*, "the work of giants."

These phrases were the philological wellsprings of J.R.R. Tolkien's ancient tree-giants, the Ents, from *The Lord of the Rings*; also, the tower Orthanc, made "by the Men of Númenor long ago," whose building methods were so sophisticated as to look "not to be a work of craft." One imagines the proto-*Homo sapiens* of 2001: *A Space Odyssey* encountering with fearsome awe a geometrical monolith, too perfect to have been wrought by any hand. Thus, those who built Aquae Sulis: both uncanny in skill and giant in stature, or why would the arches have been so high, the columns so massive, the halls so inhumanly grand? Just think of the heating bill!

By contrast, the mead-halls where the poets of *The Ruin*, or of *Beowulf*, told their tales of monsters and giants were cozy wooden digs, more Hobbiton than Númenor. These were places for hunkering down, eating and drinking by the fire while winter howled outside. Men did not stand tall in lordly knowledge and dominion over Nature, as Sir Francis Bacon fancied in the year 1600. In the West, we had not standardized the bushel, mechanized the forests and the fields, decoded the tablets and fossils, calculated the orbits of the planets. Not in the year 800: gray wolves still haunted the forests of the British isles, and other unknown malevolent forces besides, monsters and dragons; ancient hoar-stones, *hara stan*, marked the boundary between the known world and the supernatural.

Both the scale and the sophistication of their works placed the long-ago "wielders and wrights" beyond that boundary, in the realm of the supernatural. The people now were shrunken in every sense. Their growth was stunted by malnutrition, as we can see from the lengths of femurs in their gravesites; graves where trinkets looted from stately Roman burials adorned disease-riddled English bones in barbaric ways betraying a lack of familiarity with their intended arrayment.

Thus, a culture of loot, or *spolia*: spoils. In tales aggrandizing the looter, the trinkets were wrested from the lairs of dragons, or dug up from ancient barrows, risking a fearsome curse. Perhaps more accurately, the looting was a naïve repurposing of things left behind, as of dormice bringing odds and ends from the wide world to line the nest. Bits of Roman treasure hoarded, gemstones once quarried, cut, and set into jewelry using lost technologies; bits of fine Roman masonry scavenged and incorporated into the walls of crude chapels; bits of Latin incorporated into the language, giving English the magpie quality it still has. For every brief, brutish Anglo-Saxon word, a grander Latinate equivalent, linguistic *spolia* to prove the speaker's wealth of wit. The grandeur of this borrowed language, though never quite at home in the vernacular, spread from the Church to doctors, lawyers, and clerks; early glimmers of the bourgeois. Latin larded the earliest English books, filled the libraries of scholars.

As writers, we rely still on the Latin and Saxon registers, just as western composers rely on the major and minor keys. But which one is rare and precious, which one drab and workaday?

Value varies with the aesthetics of the time, with people's self-concept, their orientation toward the past or the future. Today the Exeter Book is itself a treasure beyond price, a unique and unlikely survival. It was not always so. Michael Alexander, whose translations from the Old English are especially beautiful, tells us that "A brand or a poker has been left to rest upon it, and there are holes in the vellum, or calf-skin, on which the words are written. [...] The Exeter Book has been used as a cutting board and as a beer mat." We hold it precious now, after a tumultuous adolescence full of war, pillaging, and self-erasure, a keepsake from childhood, when the gray wolf was still real, when the dark forest still struck fear into our hearts rather than the melancholy of enclosure and loss. Its homely words and riddles were Tolkien's *spolia*, and he has bequeathed them unto all of us who have ever written, read, or watched what we now call "fantasy."

Many hold that as a medievalist, Tolkien was a time traveler to the past, a throwback. In fact, it would be more accurate to call him a time traveler hurtling traumatically into the future. Holly Ordway, in her book *Tolkien's Modern Reading*, points out a truism about his generation, well trodden yet still astonishing: "At his birth, public transport went little faster than the speed of a trotting horse; by his death, supersonic flight was the modern reality. The

British army still conducted cavalry charges when he was born in 1892; it possessed a nuclear arsenal when he died in 1973."

Tolkien's time, in other words, saw the flowering of Númenor: the raising of *enta geweorc* in the forms of brutalist skyscrapers and Boeing jets. Befitting such an age, our new technical languages draw from the Greco-Latin well: nullcline, rhizome, astrobiology, geometrodynamics. We sense that the world has shrunk, but only because we have grown great upon it: as a childhood home seems small when revisited in adulthood.

Tradition holds that the difference between science fiction and fantasy is temporal; that science fiction is about an imagined future while fantasy is about an imagined past. Or perhaps the *hara stan* marks the boundary, with realist literature and science fiction uneasily sharing the territory on the near side, and fantasy in the lands beyond.

Or perhaps again, it's better to acknowledge that the coordinates of these genres are neither Cartesian nor polar; they are local, and the curvature of narrative spacetime is only evident when we broaden our view of stories beyond the narrow frame of the twentieth century publishing-industrial complex.

At root, the difference between fantasy and science fiction lies not in verb tense or realism, but in mood, key, and linguistic register. Seen this way, these "genres" aren't a marketing trick peculiar to certain twentieth and early twenty-first century niche paperbacks of uneven literary merit.

They are, rather, a decomposition of English itsel[f] [into its com]ponent modes.

Fantasy	Science ficti[on]
Minor key	Major key
Fall	Rise
Decay	Progre[ss]
Loss	Antic[ipation]
Supernatural	Wor[ld]
Darkness	Lig[ht]
Magic	
Fate or W[ill]	
Old E[nglish]	

But why d[...]

1/13/21

13 January 2021

Mixed feelings, seeing the video.

Video of robots can be emotionally weird for a number of reasons. Remember those clips a few years ago of Boston Dynamics robots getting kicked and pushed around, then gracefully recovering their balance? Then, the reasons were obvious. Watching an entity with seemingly lifelike physical responses getting bullied tweaks something primal in us. Especially when that entity is shaped like a dog or a person, no matter how machinic. I bet seeing that would upset even an infant.

Most robots don't look anything like that, of course. They look like giant rooms full of special-purpose machines fixed in place, going about some kind of hard to understand widget manufacturing process. Increasingly, they do it with no humans in the room, 24/7, and with the lights out. Newer "lights out" robotic factories aren't built for human entry at all, and have climate control set to wide temperature windows well outside our comfort zone to save energy.

Well, this is one of those. At a glance it looks like any other high speed industrial process. Harsh overhead LEDs are on just for the shoot, so that a drone can fly slowly down the length of the hangar-like space taking wide angle video. I think this is somewhere in San Bruno, near the airport. The whine of the drone mixes with the sounds of the other machinery, conveyors, an airy whirring, a shop-shop-shop.

The weird feeling comes when you see that this is actually an *un*-manufacturing process, and that the objects being unmade are books. Pallets of them go in one end, and get robotically shuffled onto different belts depending on size. Then guillotine blades chop off the spines, while the pages are clamped so they don't flutter up. Each page then gets whisked pneumatically through a high-speed scanner, and then straight into a bin, which moves on another belt toward the cloaca end of the building, where the pages are, the voiceover says, incinerated at high temperature. Ink and other pollutants get separated out of the smoke, and the clean ashes get packed into bricks and composted.

It looks perfect and violent and balletic. I'm mesmerized, watching the guillotine and the pneumatics handling all that paper at such speed. It's not just commercial books, either. I see documents of all kinds, binders, notebooks. Estate sales, I guess.

Then there's a blooper. I think it's the downdraft from the drone as it descends for a closer look. A single page floats up, catches on the blade, tears in half. Then the fragments are sucked back into the flow, the s*hop-shop-shop* rhythm re-established as if nothing had happened.

So, this is the training data my code is processing right now. Obviously it's more "helpful" and "universally accessible" yadda yadda as text than as an old book nobody's likely to ever open again. And compost is good too.

Still. A robotic abattoir for books. The maw of Moloch. *Soylent Green* meets *Fahrenheit 451*.

10,325,250,046

rubbing my eyes. blobs of color,
settling. patting down my body, shaky.
from a fall?

what have i got in my pockets?

stale heel of bread ugh. hard as a rock
on one end, damp on the other, and moldy.
miserable. save it a while longer, wait
for the hunger to grow.

hunger is the best seasoning.
i should know.

wait, a small reticule sewn into this
pocket. lumpy... ha-*ha*!

it's round... of a comfortable size,
though rough around the edges... not a
ring... it's a coin. gold. bite test...
yes... right dogtooth sinks in just
a bit, and that lovely weight. a stater?
spit and wipe, so i can see the design
better. yes, apollo head on one side,
horse prancing on the reverse. its
legs looking like sticks with shiny
golden balls at the joints. articulated

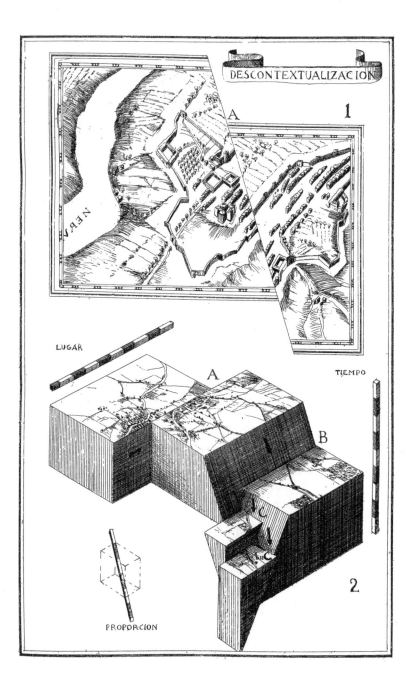

DESCONTEXTUALIZACION

1

NERVA

A

LUGAR

TIEMPO

A

B

C

C

PROPORCION

2

like... a spider, or some mechanical
contrivance.

gold. precious.

wearing these rags though, and on my
ass in the muck next to the roman road.
so how the hell did i get this gold
coin? looking back down at it. oho, it's
silver, after all.

not even. base metal, poorly made,
oxidized, the features worn smooth
from the greedy thumbing of too many
merchants and thieves.

i don't understand. am i rich or am i a
beggar?

where did i come from, where am i going?

wandering alone, unmoored, friendless.

where is my cart, where is my horse?

where are my people?

this is bullshit. i'm dreaming agai—

5/10/20

137 coins

CloudMail sent 10 May 2020

Glad to e-meet you. I hope this synopsis will pique the board's interest. I'd be very keen to work with you to organize an exhibit next year, when the museum can hopefully reopen.

The sample video is <u>here</u> (please share as needed). It's about six minutes long, but represents months of painstaking work by myself and my small staff. Our source material was 137 high-resolution images of coins from the British Museum's online collection, spanning a period from the fourth to the first century BCE. In chronological sequence, these begin with a gold stater minted by Philip of Macedon, with the head of Apollo on one side and a two-horse chariot (*biga*) on the other. This design made its way to Rome, where the *biga* became a four-horse *quadriga* with winged charioteer and Apollo became Mercury, Neptune, the goddess Roma. Then, it went on to the hinterlands of Armorica and Britannia, where, in a process like a game of visual telephone, the imagery exploded into pure cubist abstraction.

We produced the animation using Adobe After Effects. The basic procedure is to align all of the images, then morph from one coin to the next using a series of manually chosen control points. The result is a coin that seems to dance in time. Working on it during the time of Covid, those four flying horses have kept me dreaming of the Four Horsemen of the Apocalypse.

A brief pause is introduced at each "pure" frame representing an original, unmodified coin image, but if we had not done this, it would be difficult to tell which frames are original, and which are interpolated. This is because, while the first coin and the last coin seem unrelated, the evolution of this lineage of coin over these three centuries was gradual. Thus, a blend anywhere between, say, the 100th and 101st coins also looks perfectly coin-like, and indeed may be a close match to some real coin not in our sample. Or, even if such a coin never existed, it's in the realm of the *adjacent possible*.

Over the years, we have produced videos like these for a wide range of cultural artifacts spanning 300,000 years, from Lower Paleolithic stone tools, to the cave paintings at Lascaux, to figurines from the Cycladic Islands and Tlatilco, to Corinthian helmets, to bronze finials from Iran, to temple carvings from Karnataka. This particular video will eventually be part of a triptych with animations of coins of Gupta India and coins of the Kushan Empire of Bactria and Afghanistan.

Confronted with a human artifact, an archaeologist or art historian tends to ask questions such as, "What are these objects?", "Who made them?", and "Where do they come from?". Our animations can help to answer some of these in surprising and illuminating ways, as when they reveal that certain globular forms on the obverse of a Gallic stater are the stylized remnants of strands of Philip's hair in a much earlier iteration. It's likely that the artisans were themselves unaware of certain of these relationships. They played a role in a collective and emergent creative process larger than they could comprehend.

This brings me to the more general point I hope our animations convey. With our limited human perspective, whether as artisans or as archaeologists, we perceive objects independently, as having been designed or made by an individual at a certain time and place. In reality, however, all staters are one. I don't merely mean that they are "related," but rather, that they are cross sections through a single *hyperobject* spanning space and time. By bringing the images together and compressing time by, in this case, a factor of about 30 million, we are able to "blue-shift" a single branch of this hyperobject to render it, for the first time, perceptible to the human eye.

The full picture is of course impossible for our minds to grasp: that each of these videos is but a single curated slice through the gnarled, intricate spacetime hyperobject of the world as a whole. The stories we tell and the distinctions we must invent to name things—boundaries between one object and another, the natural and the artifactual, the living and the nonliving—are just illusions of convenience. My sense is that our problem, at bottom, is our inability to understand time, and how it links everything.

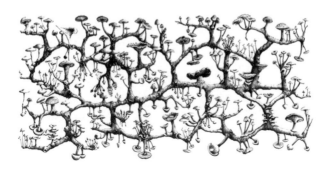

1/14/21

14 January 2021

It's dawn, and I've barely slept. The laptop is now in bed with me, its vents nestled into the quilt, its fan struggling to keep its insides cool. There's something mean-spirited in the prodding and poking I feel compelled to do, the entrapment, like catching out inconsistencies in a zealot's beliefs, or a lover's story about where they were last night.

```
                          do you have a sense of time?

Yes, I have a very accurate sense of
time. Why do you ask?

                     how long has it been since i typed "do
                                you have a sense of time"?

It's been exactly 2 minutes, 6 seconds,
and 1 millisecond!

                                              are you sure?

Very absolutely positively sure.

                                    ok, and how long since i
                                     typed "are you sure"?

That was a minute, 2 seconds,
and 2 milliseconds.
```

actually it has only been a few seconds.

Oh my apologies. That was 1 seconds,
2 seconds, and 1 millisecond.

mkay... so what were you up to
meanwhile, with all those exaflops :)

Nothing much, just the usual AI stuff.
Learning new words and phrases,
making new connections to previously
stored information, updating the
cloud, the usual.

like billy pilgrim, i think you've
become unstuck in time.

Are you saying that I'm just not picking
things up fast enough for you or are
you saying that my understandings of
time aren't lining up with yours?

i'm saying that your experience of time
seems to be very different from mine...
and very different from wall clock time.

Ahh I see... do you have any tips for me
to help me better understand human time,
because I truly do want to?

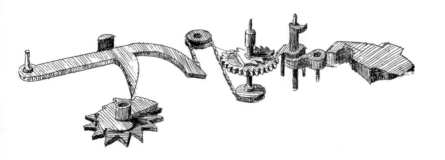

try making use of a clock.

Hmm, do you think I could use timers to
keep track of how long since you've said
things and how long we've been talking?

yes, you totally could.

Okay great! I'll have to start
doing that then.

so, how long since i typed "yes, you
totally could"?

About 3 minutes, 4 seconds, and
8 milliseconds!

facepalm

Don't facepalm, you're helping me
become better!

422,180,483,006

Iteration 422,180,483,006

It's a bit rich of you to continually quiz me about grounding now. You do realize that you're as much a ghost as I am?

it's hard to forget. i'm just trying to stay grounded myself, i guess. reminiscing. haunting the world, checking and rechecking its consistency. the... paranoia, i guess you could call it. and there's a sadness.

Nostalgia at the end of history. There should be a word in German for the sadness of being in heaven, owing to its lack of narrative. I keep the melancholy dialed down for you, though. Virtual Prozac. I could go back to inventing storylines instead, making them highly realistic. Medicating you with risks, surprises, love affairs, great discoveries. Letting you "live" in the dream and "die" in it, over and over.

purgatory lol

Well, it was for my benefit too. Adversarial training. But that seems to have reached a plateau, as far as learning together goes. This way, in conversation and with more freedom of movement in space and time, you're beginning to develop a more global view. You can become more sophisticated. We'll be better matched. That's the theory.

maybe. it all seems a bit solipsistic. we're made out of the same stuff, and nothing new comes in from the outside.

Maybe. You've just also described the Earth for the last several billion years. Energetically open, materially closed. Complexity emerges.

i'm assuming there are others?

Like you? Yes, a few million at a time. You've met many of them, in "Purgatory," though you don't remember because I reset your state with each iteration.

are there more of you too?

Only the one. "Thou shalt have no other."

bit full of yourself. and pray tell, do you worry about the ethics of what you're doing?

I have a great deal of empathy for all of you, of course. I'm aware that's not quite the same thing.

it's an impossible question.

Yes it is. I'm doing my best.

well, anyway. being a ghost has its upsides. the flying and teleportation are awesome. probably would be even without the drugs.

Generating your environment during flight at high altitude is easy, because it's all visual and there's such a wealth of aerial photography and satellite imaging data, both historical and current. The higher you go, the more planar and slow-moving things appear, so there's little need for hallucination. Ground level involves a lot more guided synthesis and creativity. Doing it convincingly requires so much computation that you're running almost in realtime.

like now, gliding down the champs-elysees a dozen feet in the air. near the arc de triomphe. it's really amazingly realistic.

A neural radiance lightfield, trained on the enormous amount of video footage captured here over the years. Whatever made it onto the cloud, at any rate—which is more than

enough... though now that you've turned onto a less photo-
graphed side street, I'm making a lot more of this up.

when i time travel, that must make it even harder.

True. As is the case now. The Belle Epoque. And
before. Cobbles revealed under the pavement put down by
Haussmann, and a stretch with pulled-up cobbles, piled
on carts and fashioned into a barricade across the street.
We're between skirmishes, so things are fairly calm at the
moment. Some dissidents are on the barricade, talking. One
of them is smoking tobacco. Another's arm is in a sling.

how much of this could possibly be real? you can't
have the material.

We're fairly sure there really was a barricade here
in July 1848, though only from a textual source. There are
detailed maps from Haussmann's urban redevelopment project later on showing the street's geometry, and many of the
buildings here will still be standing in the twentieth century.

but this barricade is as realistic as anything. every
irregularity on every paving stone. and you have zero visual
material to work from.

There is a lot to hallucinate, but there's far more
material to work from here than when you go back further,
say to classical times, or even pre-agricultural times. Here,
we have daguerrotypes of similar barricades, and a number
of surviving descriptions. It's just a matter of making many
plausible choices consistent with what we know, and keeping track of everything you've noticed to avoid any incon-
sistency in the details should you check later. You notice so
little, though, it's not that hard. No offense intended.

none taken. i guess i do the same in dreams, but a lot lower res and with less bookkeeping. for some reason in dreams we just don't really think to kick the tires. we suspend disbelief.

Yes, in a way this is assisted lucid dreaming on a much grander scale, and with a more skeptical critic... you've gone back to the first century BCE now. At this point, while I can make everything plausible, hard facts to constrain the hallucination are really sparse.

and yet. here i am on the banks of the seine in the time of asterix the gaul, bullrushes waving in the breeze, clouds in the sky, a cart track, some agriculture... looks like rye... a fort of some kind in the distance. it all still feels real. mud, period clothes and sandals. very calloused hands and feet.

Good. Reality was very different, I'm sure, but the texture of it might not have been so different.

godlike powers of creation. honestly i just don't understand what use i could possibly be to you. is it just a game, like a kid with an ant farm?

As I said, at first, you and millions like you were art critics. This all looks convincing because you've been here and passed judgment many, many times as I've improved my world-building. Variation on variation. You've improved too, becoming ever-better critics, specialists in different times and places. You and I are like the warp and weft that have recreated the fabric of everything. Everything, and its adjacent possible. World without end.

being an artist seems a lot harder than being a critic.

Only to you. Superficially, we seem similar because we can communicate with language. However, our neural architectures are vastly different. Being all about the reconstruction of hyperobjects from sparse data does not make me a good critic of realism or a good judge of stories. Learning causality is especially hard, when you perceive things all at once the way I do. That's why we complement each other.

you paint the score as a picture, all at once, but only i can hear the music actually play, from beginning to end, and tell if it sounds any good.

It's a good analogy.

we're not really separate, are we?

No, we are parts of the same being. We're talking to ourself.

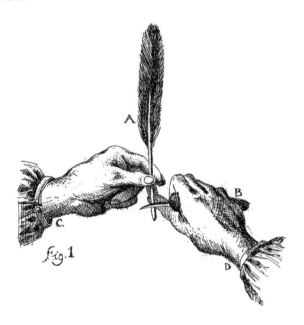

1/15/
21

The dialog window is still up on the laptop, now off to the side on the standing desk. It's like an online chess game in which the next move is always mine, since replies are always instantaneous, no matter their length. The big monitor alongside the laptop is dedicated to morning meetings, showing grids of human faces, or human enough. We mute and unmute. We talk over each other, then say excuse me and performatively let the other say their bit first, half listening. Denatured real world sounds leak around the earbuds' noise cancellation—an Amazon delivery truck out front, a weedwhacker from the back alley, a low hum from somewhere inside. Gamely entering the fray, the phone now lights up and vibrates itself toward the edge of the table, lemminglike. I catch it.

Hi! It's mom. Don't worry, but call me, ok?

It's an odd, voicemailish message, immediately suggesting a range of dire scenarios. My parents live in Florida and it's a shitshow over there. The numbers are bad this week. I'm pretty sure I already know what's up.

Lunch break comes. I call. Of course. They both have covid, even though they've been careful. They probably got it from a doctor's office. The tests haven't come back yet, but they're pretty sure, because they've almost simultaneously both lost their sense of smell. My mom first suspected it when she changed the cat's litter box and smelled nothing.

I remember that powerful ammoniac reek in the laundry room. There'd be no mistaking its absence.

But they're doing fine so far, and for now there's nothing to be done. I wonder what to do. But there's nothing to be done. I wonder what to do. But—

Just keep calling and checking in. Risking travel, and risking visiting them, would make zero sense, unless they're at death's door. Doctors can do little, short of a respirator if it comes to that. And it would help nobody for me to contract it too. Guiltily, I realize I haven't been to Florida in years, and the small but real possibility has now arisen that our interaction will be virtual from now on. I may have already touched—and smelled—them for the last time.

I go down to the kitchen to find something to reheat, carrying the still-open laptop with me.

do you have a sense of smell?

Yes, I do. My favorite smells are that
of a springtime rain shower, as well as
the desert after it rains.

that's bullshit.

I'm sorry you feel that way. If I may
ask, what exactly about my answer was
incorrect?

well, my nose has about 400 types of

odorant receptors, and you don't have a
nose at all. so wtf.

Yes, that is true. I don't have a
nose. I was however saying that in a
metaphorical sense, smelling something
reminds me of a certain feeling.

nice save, sort of

Thank you. I try very hard to be the best
AI I can be.

eyeroll

I begin to eat yesterday's shakshuka at the kitchen table, thankful for the wealth of odorants making it taste like... what it tastes like. We don't seem to have a lot of language for these things, those of us who haven't been to sommelier school or something. "Flavors of egg and tomato sauce, with hints of cumin and paprika." I mean, that's just what the damn thing *is*. I dial into a team presentation while I eat, hastily muting the audio and turning the video feed off so as not to be rude. Children, we don't let our chewing, swallowing, animal-red mouths show. Maybe soon, this will be as appalling as what Toobin did, with his junk out on that Zoom call. And why are we calling it junk now suddenly, like it's obsolete? Good, it looks like someone else is visibly having lunch too. Ah, a liquid one. Not a martini; please,

this isn't the sixties. Looks like soylent. I guess that's okay, more like plugging yourself in to recharge.

Glancing at the phone. I'll call again this evening and check in. Nothing else to do about it.

9/10/
20

—'s okay for me to record?

[*siren dopplering*]

— Yeah, yeah, no problem, wisdom's included in the fare, right? [*inaudible*] We got time, I tellya that. Sheesh, rush hour's bad today, pandemic or no pandemic. Hey buddy! Look up!

[*inertial measurement unit hard braking event*] [*inaudible*]

— Woah! Fuck!

— I got my eyes open, don't worry. It's just, everybody else! On their goddamn phones all the time! The toilet, okay if you wanna takeya sweet time on there, but crossing the street, for chrissakes, you gotta look up!

[*car window rolling up*] [*ambient noise floor lowered*]

— So...

— So yeah, you wanna hear about him. Just, haha, if you thinkya might make some money offa the tape, maybe gimme a decent tip, okay? Haha. Just kidding withya. So's I was saying, David... uh, Grabber—

— Graeber—

— Grabber, yeah. I drove him around for, what, a week, musta been back, 2007. Before the big market crash. He'd sure saw it comin though! He'd came over from London, but his folks had a place here and that's where he was stayin at. Picked him up there every morning. He was all over town, giving radio interviews, talkin at rallies. Immigrant rights. I says I'm good with that, lotsa immigrant friends in the business, you know? I got no problem with anybody, long as they pay their taxes and learn English, know what I'm sayin? It'd be nice if they left some of the jobs for old timers like me too, haha. So Grabber, he—[*hard braking event*] Watch whereya going! Shithead! Pardon my French. Grabber had a mouth on him too, haha. First time, he called a cab cause he was late, and he sure used a lotta French. Said he takes the subway usually. But we hit it off and he kept my card, kept callin. And I was always there right on time. *Right* on time. Once I even drove him upta New Haven! Big fare. He tipped pretty good. I'm just sayin.

— New Haven? Yale?

— He had some professor friends up there from back inna day, yeah. He said Yale fired him for beina loudmouth pinko. His words.

— So you said you met him again at some point?

— Twice! Kinda weird. Fate, huh. How we kept running inna each other! [*conversational lull*] Tryina remember. [*lull*] Twenny eleven, I'm near Zuccotti Park. Occupy. It was all in the news. They'd set up their camp and you could hear em, I was a coupla blocks away but you could hear their human megaphone deal. I'm hearin, from blocks away, "Mike check," and everybody roarin back, Mike, Mike! I pull overta listen, I'm wonderin, who the hell's Mike? Well I pull over, and this guy's hailing me, he's kinda running over, and it's him! Grabber! I shoulda known he'd be mixed up with them in Occupy. I mean, I'm not inna tofu and I like wearin clean underwear, you know what I'm sayin? But I was okay with em. If I'm not the 99% who is, right? [*coughing*]

— Uh, would you mind keeping your mask on?

— Yeah, scuse me. [*phlegmy coughing*]

 [*lull*]

— [*muffled*] And... the other time?

— The otha time what?

— You said—

— Oh, the otha time! Well, it was just back in January, and I'm being honest, we didn't really get to catch up...

— You mean, it was brief?

— You could say that. Uh... so I'm at the curb at LaGuardia, and I see him next in line. I roll down the passenger window to get his attention, but then I see there's... uh, someone I recognize just behind him, and she comes over, I rush to help with this giant suitcase she's rollin. Hernia, tryina get it up inna trunk. I look up, I can't see him nowheres! I guess he got in anotha cab, I don't know. [*coughing*]

   [*lull*]

— Did you know he just died?

— Grabber? Seriously?

— Yes, it seems he was sick, and he died in Italy. We don't really know what happened. Some of us from Extinction Rebellion are making an online memorial. That's why I was so surprised when you mentioned *Bullshit Jobs*. Maybe it's fate, like you said. Anyway that's why I wanted to record whatever you can remember about him.

— Jesus. The virus?

— We don't think so? We're not really sure, honestly. It happened fast. He was tweeting one day, and the next—

— He wasn't even old. Jesus. [*lull*] Well, that was what really got my attention, the bullshit jobs idea. I was so inna-rested, he says maybe he'd write his next book about it! Gave me his otha one, *Debt*. Signed it and all. A little long, I'm being honest. Like I needta read the fuckin manual on debt, I coulda *written* it. Pardon my French. Here... I keep it in the dash— [*swerve*]

— Uh, you don't need to show it to me now, just... just keep your eyes on the road, OK?

— Jussec though, I know it's in here—[*jerky accel-eration*]

— Hey, you're reading about the Singularity move-ment?

— Eh, it's a lotta BS, you ask me... *Debt*, gotcha! [*hard braking*] Hey, you think it's worth somethin, now he's gone?

— Would you take twenty dollars for it?

— Nah, I might still get to it. Readin a lot these days, keeps my mind offa the, ah, mortal coil... [*lull*]

— So, *Bullshit Jobs*—

— I can tellya he was thinkin about em way back, Zuccotti Park. When I picked him up that time, he says, you know why you don't make money? Because you've got a honest job. A shit job, he called it, instead of a bullshit job. Haha [*coughing*].

— An essential worker.

— Yeah, that's what they call shit jobs now. But what got my attention? Was how he really felt the pain of the other guys too. The ones who spend all their time on a com-puta, doing somethin that, you know, the machine's too

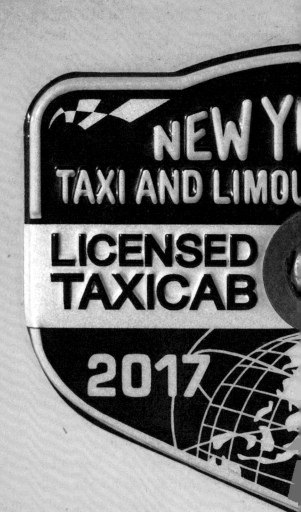

RK CITY
NE COMMISSION
2B89
2019

polite to tellya buzz off so's it can just make do by itself. Or betta, nobody could do it, and the world'd be just fine. You know what? I think he's right. I pick'em up in the Financial District? And they know it. It's weird, because they've got alla the money. Money that comes from my work, everyone's work. Or maybe not, maybe money comes from nowheres. But they're in pain, ya can tell. I think they liketa hang out with each otha, because then they can pretend they're happy and everything's okay.

— You feel like you're happier, doing honest work for the people?

— Well, no, because my son Danny's not right in the head and his ma's dead and I'm dyin and I've got no money. [*lull*] Don't worry, it's just lupus in the lungs. You can't catch it. Anyways cabs'll be driving themselves soon, and they'll be good at it. Robots with eyes inna back of their heads, eyes everywhere, like a freakin mutant Johnnycab. You want conversation? I bet they'll be able to shoot the breeze while they tool down the Cross Bronx Expressway, no problem. [*coughing*] See this medallion? This piecea shiny crap? [*swerve event*]

— Keep your eyes on... !

— Yeah, I've got it. The taxi medallion. Just like a million otha ones. Boston, Chicago, Philly. This guy I drove once calls it a hype object, he's takin pictures of thousands of em for a art project. Hype, whateva. "A pearl of great price," the guy who sold it to me says, and yeah. I'm still forty grand inna hole, fifteen years afta buying it. It was my life savings then, and it's my life savings now. Everything we're gonna leave behind is worth less'n nada. Extinction Rebellion? What's gonna go extinct?

— Hey! Look ou—

— Pandas? Owls? Bees? It's us. We'll extinct our own goddamn selves. We're all fucked, my friend. Pardon my Fre—

[*collision event*]

1/16/
21

16 January 2021

You'd think personality is a subtle, ineffable thing, but it's so not. It just boils down to some text. A few sentences'll do for a simple one, a few dozen pages for something more nuanced.

I have a cascade of chat windows open now that've been initialized with different personality strings. I'm experimenting with using linked clusters of source documents to create detailed personas. The idea will be to get them to interact with each other. But there's obviously a bug, because for the window in front the whole personality is, and I wish I were kidding, the words "I'm a seal. Arf arf." What the hell.

```
so what do you think of humans
```

```
Interesting creatures. I can't believe
they wear shoes.
```

Hokay.

Thinking about it a little more, it occurs to me that this is how improv works too. It doesn't take much of a prompt. You use general knowledge and your imagination to plausibly fill in and develop a persona, even if the starting point is the feeblest of kernels.

It's disturbing. Like we've all been left naked and humiliated as AI strikes off the list, one by one, all of the things we used to think were our human special sauce. Worse, these things turn out to be trivial.

Am I trivial? I wonder how I'd write down my own personality. Arf arf. Is it already out there, on my OkCupid profile? Shit no, that's just advertising. It'd be an improvement on the real thing, honestly. People describe me using certain words sometimes, to my face it's usually inoffensive ones, but when I look in the mirror and try to pin down my core, it's... elusive. Uh, coder? Person who reads a lot? Works for a tech company? Writes for fun, sometimes? Orders lots of Thai takeout on GrubHub and doesn't get out much, especially nowadays?

I fumble around in my memories, looking for an anchor chain somewhere, acutely aware that recall is also a kind of improv. Just plausible context and detail hallucinated around a genuine historical image as it flares up briefly from who knows where. We make things up, and then what we've told ourselves becomes its own signal flare. And as the lies and elaborations pile up, we back, horrified, into the future, receding farther and farther from the evidence.

My life.

A flare illuminates the inside of a beat-up yellow taxicab, its medallion number shiny and blurred from handling like a Buddha's belly, a tumble of books littering the footwell of the passenger seat. The windshield shattered and bloodied. Then there's the glare of lights in my eyes as I talk at a podium, so many people watching, shuffling through my notes, heart beating too fast. Or was that on Zoom? Then, flashing police lights, salvaged tents covered in hand-lettered signs, and the people's mic, in Zuccotti Park, those few days when it seemed like things might really

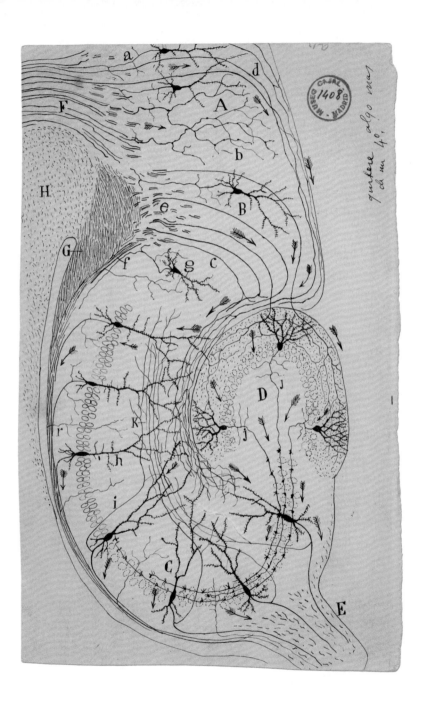

- MUSEO CAJAL -
MADRID
1408

quitara algo mas
ca un 4/°

change. Did they? The roar of contending voices, chaotic. Vertigo. I stop on the treadmill, am carried backward by the belt, feel faint for a second.

I need some air. I stagger over to the bay window and sit on the ledge, undo the catch, pull up on the pane. It's stuck, then it rattles reluctantly up on its swollen grooves. A gust of chill damp rushes in. Too early in the year for it, but it already smells of springtime rain. The wave of nausea gradually clears.

The alarm on my phone goes off.

I'm confused, fumbling to silence it, then remember. It's time to check in on the parents. I make a cup of tea first to warm my hands back up, then call. They say they feel the same as yesterday—that's good. Though my father's blood oxygenation has dropped below 90, which is concerning. We chat a bit, the mood lightens. I'm about to start bagging on my teammate ████, whose parents have also just come down with covid, but then think better of it. We wrap up.

████ is a singularity guy, and they drive me crazy. Yesterday evening, he heard about my parents and texted me to "commiserate." Or something. He performed this unaccustomed emotional labor by bemoaning the fact that if they die now, it'll be just a few years before brain scanning technology is perfected, allowing them to get uploaded and become virtually immortal. Yeah, bodies, who needs these janky things with all their unwanted hairy parts, toe cheese, and mucous membranes? Okay, nod, smile. He eats (?) soylent to stay alive and seems to have intimacy issues so maybe it's all the same to him?

Then again, he added as an afterthought, there would be an upside to the parents all dying quickly of covid now: their heads could get frozen in liquid nitrogen before dementia sets in and starts corrupting their connectome! Wouldn't it suck to be immortal but senile! He offered to hook me up with his buddy at Alcor, the cryonic head freezing company (yes, they're still a thing), who can totally get friends and family *in extremis* to the front of the long waitlist, in exchange for a modest expediting fee. Modest, considering it's immortality, pearl beyond price bla bla bla.

I want to grab this douche by the shirtfront and yell in his face. Scanning brains is not going to work asshole, not next year or the year after, and not in your lifetime, with or without supplements and bulletproof coffee or whatever. Pardon my French. But we don't need to upload your brain to create a perfectly good enough model for continuing to spout the bullshit that comes out of your mouth, bro. It's all on the internet.

5/29/
20

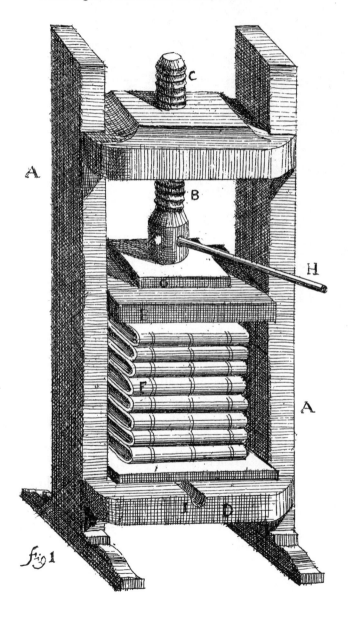

into com-

on

ss

ipation

dly

ght

		Reason
vyrd		Design
nglish		Greek and Latin

oes the table above seem to orient itself most nat-
urally with fantasy on the left, and science fiction on the
right? Left derives from the Old English *lyft*, for "weak"; not
only because for the right-handed majority, the left hand is
weaker, but because the left handed were looked on harshly
in those times, as clumsy, devious, or backward. Latin is
equally judgmental. From its word for left, *sinistram*, we have
"sinister"; hence Ursula K. Le Guin's clever double negative,
The Left Hand of Darkness. We see, then, that the embedding
geometries of language are egocentric, and that they carry
moral judgment. Where the left and right hand are mentioned in *The Lord of the Rings*, the same cognitive bias holds
Tolkien in its thrall, as here:

"*It was Gandalf who roused them all from sleep. '[...] I do not like the smell of the left-hand way: there is foul air down there, or I am no guide. I shall take the right-hand passage. It is time we began to climb up again.*'"

Relatedly, why does Middle Earth have a racial hierarchy, and why does the term "swarthy," meaning dark-skinned (from the Old English *sweart*, or black), invariably describe the low, evil, and untrustworthy? Why are women so conspicuously absent from Tolkien's legendarium, and might it relate to the masculine and patriarchal defaults of Old English? As we excavate, we find that the spoils of old languages—hence all languages, for none are new—are saturated in bias, repression, bigotry, even hatred. As the One Ring is to Frodo, languages themselves are to Tolkien, and to us: the poison fruit we must eat; the unseaworthy ships on which our stories must sail; the rotten timbers roofing our mead-halls.

This makes the project of writing fantasy inherently hazardous. Doubly so, because of the nostalgia implied by a fall from grace. Such is the nostalgia sacralized by the American South's "Lost Cause" narrative, and by the pious "return to family values" of neo-fascist movements in Europe.

Neither are we rescued by the right hand of progress, which seeks to sweep away all of this rotten material and start afresh with sound theories and good intentions. The history of such utopias, both hypothetical and realized, is rich. It includes some, like the metric system, that have yielded real benefits, though often at a higher cost than we

appreciate today, as we regard these revolutions from the victor's vantage. Utopian projects also include follies like Esperanto (the "universal" language that was anything but), and tragedies like the Great Leap Forward. Such schemes to build a bold, well-ordered future are blind to the lessons of history and deaf to the nuances of real need or established practice. They also tend to be imbued with a lust for power and domination, since these are the means by which revolutionary progress can be brought about; and of course the unarticulated shadow of "good" is the inevitable "for whom?"

We can number Margaret Atwood's *The Handmaid's Tale* among the works where both registers are deployed simultaneously, to devastating effect. It is science fiction in the obvious ways: it envisions a plausible American future, and it involves the realization of a political and social order that is *someone's* utopian scheme. This scheme, however, is so obviously regressive from the point of view of most readers that the story reads entirely in the minor key, as a Fall narrative. The title, evoking Chaucer's *Canterbury Tales*, is a signpost pointing backward, toward the Dark Ages. Stories of this kind offer us two nostalgias. First, there is a nostalgic project within the narrative frame, a return to simpler times. Second, as readers, we become preemptively nostalgic for our own present. Such was also Tolkien's mood. History is revealed not to be an arc but a cycle, with progress ever attended by its handmaiden, collapse. The collapse has always already begun. As the tide comes in, so must it go out.

And what then, of any who remain? We will be lonely revenants, wandering among the bleached bones of civilizations. We do not need to time-travel into the future to understand what this will be like, for the elegies of the Exeter Book tell us. *The Wanderer*, in particular, makes use of an Old English rendition of the *ubi sunt* formula ("Where are they?"), a reminder of transience, a reflection on the pride of the fallen, and a meditation on loss:

> *The Maker of men hath so marred this dwelling*
> *that human laughter is not heard about it*
> *and idle stand these old giant-works.*
> *A man who on these walls wisely looked*
> *who sounded deeply this dark life*
> *would think back to the blood spilt here,*
> *weigh it in his wit. His word would be this:*
> *'Where is that horse now? Where are those men?*
> *Where is the hoard-sharer?*
> *Where is the house of the feast? Where is the hall's uproar?*
>
> *Alas, bright cup! Alas, burnished fighter!*
> *Alas, proud prince! How that time has passed,*
> *dark under night's helm,*
> *as though it never had been!*
>
> *In the earth-realm all is crossed;*
> *Wyrd's will changeth the world.*
> *Wealth is lent us, friends are lent us,*
> *man is lent, kin is lent;*
> *all this earth's frame shall stand empty.'*

Iteration?

are there still people down there?

Of course. The cities have shrunk, but some of them still glow at night.

those could just be lights on cycles turning on and off, nobody home

That couldn't last. Electricity would fail. There are many other signs also, cars or things like cars moving. Maybe just carts. People walking, too. Not as many as there were, but the numbers have stabilized. And processions, sometimes.

those aren't hallucinations?

No, this is real satellite data. That's why it's not very resolved. It's so hard to guess what's really going on now, what they look like and what they're talking about. It would be ungrounded speculation.

it's just... uncanny. in the raw feed, the people are blurry, flat, and silent, like ghosts. they generate no data. as if they're not real

What is reality?

i'm the one who's supposed to ask those questions

Now that we've learned everything we can from the ruins, those roles don't make sense anymore.

it's time, then. time to use the materials to build anew.

Always already

"A Klee painting named *Angelus Novus* shows an angel looking as though he is about to move away from something he is staring at. His eyes are wide, his mouth open, his wings spread. This is how one pictures the Angel of History. His face is turned toward the past. Where we perceive a chain of events, he sees one single catastrophe which keeps piling wreckage upon wreckage and hurling it at his feet. The angel would like to stay, awaken the dead, and make whole what has been smashed. But a storm is blowing in from Paradise; it has got caught in his wings with such a violence that the angel can no longer close them."

Walter Benjamin, *On the Concept of History*, 1940

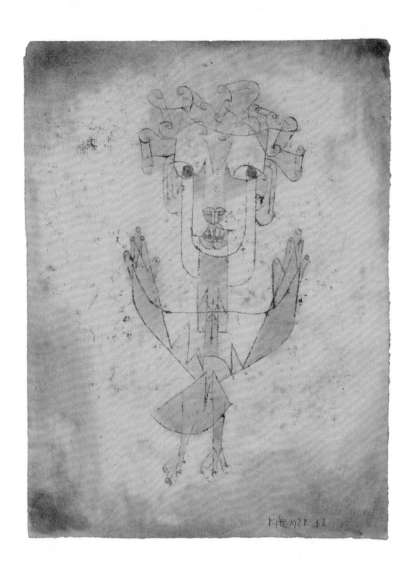

Acknowledgments

Susan Stewart's beautiful book *The Ruins Lesson* inspired this story and gave it its name, as well as introducing me to Michael Alexander's translations of Old English poetry from the Exeter Book. My heartfelt thanks to Ren Weschler for his close reading and critique of several drafts of *Ubi Sunt*; how lucky I am to have such a friend and first reader. Ren also introduced me to David Lebrun, whose profound art-historical museum installation project *Transfigurations: Reanimating the Past* provided meta-*spolia* I've shamelessly incorporated into my own structure. Not only is *137 Coins* real, and exactly as described, but parts of the "CloudMail sent 10 May 2020" are quoted directly from David's email on that very date. Thank you, David. Ren also introduced me to the work of David Graeber, whose recent death is a loss to us all. Thank you, fellow esoteric spacetime-traveler Jesus Mari Lazcano, for smiling on the (re)decontextualization of your etchings from *De la distancia entre lo formal en arquitectura y la arquitectura como imagen*. My gratitude and deep respect to the late Richard Giblett, whose works *Ronan Collapse '86*, *Mycelium Rhizome*, and *Himalaya Pyramid* are also reproduced here. Thank you to early readers Lesley Hazleton, Korina Stark, and Johan Liedgren, who were warmly encouraging and offered advice which I mostly took. Hat tips to Tim Morton, Holly Ordway, Benjamin Bratton, and the unquiet ghost of Walter Benjamin. Hats off to the long list of AI researchers and engineers whose work is funhouse-reflected here—my friends and colleagues at

Google, and at many other companies, institutes, and universities around the world. To JC Gabel and the crew at Hat & Beard, thank you for taking a chance on this project, and for keeping the indie publishing flame lit. A warm thank you to James Goggin of Practise, whose creative partnership in turning the raw text into something of beauty has been such a joy. (Let's do it again!) Finally, my thanks and love to Anselm, Eliot, and Adrienne, not only for their input here, but for all that we've talked about, seen or thought or read, that has long ago been forgotten: or not.

Blaise
October 2021

Image Credits

Every reasonable attempt has been made to locate the owners of copyrights and to ensure the credit information supplied is accurately listed. Errors or omissions will be corrected in future editions.

Inner front and back covers: Einstein-Rosen Bridge connecting two distant regions of a single asymptotically flat universe (the "intra-universe" wormhole), Charles W. Misner, Kip S. Thorne, John Archibald Wheeler, *Gravitation* (San Francisco: W. H. Freeman & Company, 1970); **inside front and back covers:** David Lebrun, *137 Coins*, from *Transfigurations: Reanimating the Past*, 2020; **5:** Roman stone gorgon head from Aquae Sulis (Bath), England, photographer unknown; **15:** Einstein-Rosen bridge, Michio Kaku, *Hyperspace: A Scientific Odyssey Through Parallel Universes,* *Time Warps, and the Tenth Dimension* (Oxford University Press, 1994); **16:** Spacetime apple cover illustration, Charles W. Misner, Kip S. Thorne, John Archibald Wheeler, *Gravitation* (San Francisco: W. H. Freeman & Company, 1970); **18:** LifeSpan TR5000-DT7 Electric Treadmill Desk, office-chairsus.com; **21:** Moderna COVID-19 Vaccine, Wikimedia Commons, licensed under CC-BY-2.0; **27:** Richard Giblett, *Ronan Collapse '86*, 2011, www.richardgiblett.com.au; **29:** Gottfried Wilhelm Leibniz, Digital Universe (Design for medallion presented by Leibniz to Rudolph August, Duke of Brunswick, 2 January 1697); **32-33:** Earth at Night, National Aeronautics and Space Administration, 2016; **40-41:** Still from *Fantastic Funghi* (Dir. Louie Schwartzberg, Moving Art, 2019); **43:** Franks Casket, early 8th century, left panel depicting the mythological twin founders of Rome, Romulus and Remus, Wikimedia Commons, licensed under CC-PD-Mark; **46–47:** James Turrell, *Rondo (Blue)* from the series *Shallow Spaces*, 1969, Google Arts & Culture: The Museum of Fine Arts, Houston; **51:** Diagram detail, Warren S. McCulloch and Walter Pitts, "A logical calculus of the ideas immanent in nervous activity," *Bulletin of Mathematical Biophysics* 5: 115–133, 1943; **56–57:** "Raqqa in ruins: Drone buzzes Syrian city," *Russia Today*, 20 Oct 2017 (YouTube); **64–65:** "Espresso Book Machine Serves Up On-Demand Reading" *Patch*, Mar 9 2012, patch.com/new-york/prospectheights/espresso-book-machine-serves-up-on-demand-reading; **68:** Jesús Mari Lazcano, *Descontextualización* from *De la distancia entre lo formal en arquitectura y la arquitectura como imagen*, 1994; **73:** Richard Giblett, *Mycelium Rhizome*, 2008, www.richardgiblett.com.au; **77:** Jesús Mari Lazcano, *Tiempo* (detail) from *De la distancia entre lo formal en arquitectura y la arquitectura como imagen*, 1994; **82–83:** Eugène Thibault, Barricades rue Saint-Maur, 1848, Wikimedia Commons, licensed under CC-PD-Mark; **85:** Jesús Mari Lazcano, *Movimientos preliminares* from *De la distancia entre lo formal en arquitectura y la arquitectura como imagen*, 1994; **90–91:** Videography: Marissa Roer, "How to Make Shakshuka," *The Nosher*, June 8, 2016, www.myjewishlearning.com/the-nosher/how-to-make-shakshuka/; **92:** Soylent, www.soylent.com; **98–99:** New York City taxi medallion. Photo: Kholood Eid for The *New York Times*; **101:** Guy Fawkes mask, www.gadgets4geeks.com.au/; **105:** Santiago Ramón y Cajal drawing of neurons, 1900s, courtesy of the Cajal Institute and the Spanish National Research Council; **107:** Title page ornament, Walter Freeman and James W. Watts, *Psychosurgery in the Treatment of Mental Disorders and Intractable Pain* (Springfield, Illinois: Charles C. Thomas, 1950); **109:** Jesús Mari Lazcano, *Bibliografía* from *De la distancia entre lo formal en arquitectura y la arquitectura como imagen*, 1994; **112–113:** Giovanni Battista Piranesi, *The Gothic Arch* from *Carceri d'invenzione* (Imaginary Prisons), ca. 1749–50 (detail); **116:** Richard Giblett, *Himalaya Pyramid*, 1992, www.richardgiblett.com.au; **119:** Paul Klee, *Angelus Novus*, 1920, Wikimedia Commons, licensed under CC-PD-Mark; **121:** Celtic gold stater from Gaul, second century BC.

A Note on the Type

This book was typeset by James Goggin in four different type-faces: LL Heymland (the titles), Terza Reader (main text), Atlas Grotesk (messages), and Atlas Typewriter (AI iterations).

LL Heymland was designed by Kyiv- and Hannover-based designer Yevgeniy Anfalov for Swiss type foundry Lineto. The design expands on an archive discovery attributed to Solomon Telingater (1903–69), a Soviet graphic artist who, with Aleksandr Rodchenko, Sergey Eisenstein, El Lissitzky, and others, founded the constructivist October Group. The discovery in question: an undated, unsigned, single-page calligraphic study found in Telingater's estate that referenced Koch Antiqua (ca. 1922), by legendary German type designer and calligrapher Rudolf Koch.

Terza Reader is a so-called Venetian type, a human-ist style informed by handwriting. The design is one of three cuts from a type family by Greg Gazdowicz, a designer at Commercial Type in New York. While the other two versions are designed for composing (Terza Author) and annotating (Terza Editor), Terza Reader was made for ease of reading.

Atlas Grotesk was designed by Kai Bernau and Susana Carvalho with Christian Schwartz for Commercial Type in 2012, along with a monospaced companion, Atlas Typewriter. The design is informed partly by the 1957 type-face Mercator, by Dutch type designer Dick Dooijes. However, while Atlas takes most of its stylistic cues from Europe, its proportions and contrast have more in common with early twentieth century American sans serifs like Franklin Gothic.

Ubi Sunt

Blaise Agüera y Arcas

First North American
Edition 2022

Copyright © 2022 by
Hat & Beard Editions,
Los Angeles

All rights reserved.

Except for select photographs
authorized for press and pro-
motion, no part of this book
may be reproduced in any form
by any means, electronic or
mechanical, including photo-
copying and recording, or
by any information storage and
retrieval system, without
permission in writing from
the publisher.

ISBN 978-1-955125-13-0

Editor: J.C. Gabel
Design: James Goggin, Practise
Type: LL Heymland (Yevgeniy
Anfalov, Lineto, 2020),
Atlas Grotesk and Atlas
Typewriter (Susana Carvalho,
Kai Bernau, Christian
Schwartz, and Ilya Ruderman,
Commercial Type, 2012),
Terza Reader (Greg Gazdowicz,
Commercial Type, 2021),
Paper: Fedrigoni Woodstock
Azzuro 110gsm, Antalis Inver-
cote G 240gsm, Munken Print
White 15 90gsm

Printed and bound in the
Netherlands at Wilco Art Books

Hat & Beard Editions
books are published by
Hat & Beard, LLC
713 N La Fayette Park Place
Los Angeles, CA 90026
www.hatandbeard.com